Fancy Nancy's

Fabulous Fall Storybook Collection

This
SPLENDIFEROUS
BOOK
belongs to:

_____

Fancy Nancy's

Fabulous Fall Storybook Collection

By Jane O'Connor

Pictures based on the art of Robin Preiss Glasser

HARPER

An Imprint of HarperCollins Publishers

Table of Contents

Fancy NANCY

Halloween... or Bust!

"Halloween is so much fun," I tell Frenchy,
"because it is all about dressing up.
And that happens to be something I excel at."

11

On Halloween, you can be...

a caterpillar or
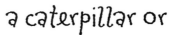

a butterfly...

12

a glittering silvery snowflake

or a Hollywood movie star...

or something completely unique.
That's a fancy way of saying one of a kind.

I am a plume-asaurus—a dinosaur that's imaginary.

Even very plain people, like my parents, get fancy on Halloween.

And we must not forget—the bonbons!
That's French for candy.

Really, what's not to love?

This year I am going to a Halloween party.
I will be a bunch of grapes
made from fuchsia balloons.

18

My friend Bree is going as a strawberry.

At the party there are many dazzling costumes.

There are robots

and pirates.

There is even a lion tamer.

Bree's costume has black sequins for strawberry seeds.
"You look spectacular," I tell her.

Bree likes my costume too.
"You even smell grape-y," she says.
"Grape bubble bath," I whisper back.

23

Soon it is time for games.
First we bob for apples.
It is very hard to do.
I pop four of my balloons.

Next we play pin the tail on the monster.
I bump into Robert's plastic sword
and *pop!* go two more balloons.

25

By the end of musical chairs,
all of my balloons have popped.

POP! POP! POP! POP! POP!

"This is disastrous!" I cry.
That is a fancy way of saying very bad.

Now I am just a brown stalk.
And brown is such a plain color.

28

29

But after some punch and many bonbons,
I feel much better.
Then I get a brilliant idea
that is both fancy and smart.

I can make myself a brand-new costume.
And I'll make it extra fancy.

I am peering out the window
of my classroom.
(Peering is a fancy word for looking.)
It has rained all week.
We can't play outside.

Ms. Glass is reading a story.

Everybody looks glum and gloomy.

(That's a fancy way to say

we are in a bad mood.)

She puts down the book.

"Class, we need something fun
to look forward to," Ms. Glass says.
"Does anyone have ideas?"
We all sit and ponder.
That means we think hard.

Clara says,

"Let's go bowling."

Robert says,

"Let's go see a movie."

Ms. Glass says,

"Those are interesting ideas.

But let's think of

something to do in school."

At home

I ponder while I pick out

a dress for tomorrow.

I never feel glum or gloomy

in this fancy dress.

Being fancy is fun.

It makes me happy.

Ooh la la!

All of a sudden

I have an idea.

My pondering has paid off!

43

The next day at school I say,

"What if we have a fancy day?

We can wear fancy clothes

and eat fancy food

and use fancy manners!"

Lionel holds up his pinkie.

"Oh, darling," he says.

"You must try the baked worms!"

Ms. Glass looks stern.

That means now is not the time

to be silly.

"I think this is a great proposal,"
Ms. Glass says.
She explains that a proposal
is like an idea.

Everybody else likes my idea too,
even Lionel.

"Next Monday will be Fancy Day,"
Ms. Glass says.

"We can start preparing now."

We make fancy place mats.

We make fancy napkin rings
from pipe cleaners.

We also make fancy crowns.

Lionel makes the points on his crown

look like bloody shark teeth.

He is such a goofball!

At snack time we put napkins

on our laps.

We chew with our mouths shut.

When Robert burps,

he says, "Pardon me."

I teach everyone how to say

thank you in French.

"It's *merci*.

You say it like this:

mair-SEE."

That evening,

I tell my family about Fancy Day.

"It was my proposal.

That means it was all my idea!"

Over the weekend
Bree and I bake cupcakes
for Fancy Day.

On Sunday night
I look through my wardrobe.
That's fancy for all my clothes.
I find my most fancy dress.
I will also wear boas, bracelets,
tons of necklaces, lace gloves,
and sparkly clips in my hair.
I am fancy all the time,
so I must be super-duper fancy
on Fancy Day.

On Monday morning
I am stunned.
(That means surprised.)
Everyone looks so posh.
But where is Ms. Glass?
Why isn't she here yet?

All of a sudden Ms. Glass rushes in.

Her tooth broke this morning.

The dentist already fixed her up.

She is fine now.

But she is not fancy.

Ms. Glass looks startled.

(That means surprised,

only in a bad way.)

"Oh no!" she cries.

"I left all my fancy stuff at home!"

We tell Ms. Glass not to feel bad.

"You can have my clips," I say.

Bree offers her boa.

Everyone helps dress up Ms. Glass.

It is like playing with a giant doll.

In no time, she is super posh.

61

Soon it is party time.

Ms. Glass says,

"We must thank Nancy for Fancy Day."

The kids all lift their cups
of lemonade.

Everybody's pinkie is up.

But no one says thank you.

They all shout, *"Merci!"*

Fancy Nancy's Fancy Words

These are the fancy words in this book:

Glum and gloomy—in a bad mood

Merci—"thank you" in French (you say it like this: mair-SEE)

Peer—look

Ponder—think hard

Proposal—an idea

Startled—surprised in a bad way

Stern—not pleased

Stunned—surprised

Wardrobe—all my clothes

I don't mean to brag,

but I am a splendid speller.

S-P-L-E-N-D-I-D.

(Splendid is even better than great.)

Bree is a splendid speller too.

We practice spelling

in our clubhouse after school.

I can even spell in French!

C-H-I-E-N means "dog."

You say it like this—SHEE-enn.

My sister is very impressed.

(Impressed means

she thinks I'm great.)

My sister cannot spell any words.

My parents spell out stuff

they don't want her to hear.

They used to fool me this way,

but not anymore.

She has to get a shot,

S-H-O-T,

at her checkup tomorrow.

At school today, Ms. Glass says,
"Our first spelling test
is on Friday."

Here is the list of test words.

pass   glass
class   happy
sad   glad
mad   peek
week   giggle

We write down the words.

Some kids make faces.

They think the words are hard.

But Bree and I are happy.

H-A-P-P-Y.

This test will be easy!

At dinner I practice some words.

"Please P-A-S-S the carrots.

May I have a G-L-A-S-S of milk?"

78

Dad claps and says, "Bravo!"

"I don't mean to brag," I say,

"but Bree and I

are the best spellers

in the C-L-A-S-S."

Later I memorize

the harder words.

(Memorize is fancy for

learn by heart.)

The hardest is "giggle."

G-I-G-G-L-E.

It has so many Gs!

I practice all week.

W-E-E-K.

It will be splendid

to spell every word right.

By Friday I am ready.

Ms. Glass says each word slowly.

The last one is "giggle."

I write down G-I-G-L-E.

Is that right?

I am not sure.

I try it another way.

G-I-G-G-L-E.

Is that right?

Then I do something wicked.

(Wicked is way worse than bad.)

I peek, P-E-E-K, at Bree's paper!

Bree has G-I-G-G-L-E.

I bet Bree is right.

I start to fix my word.

I want to get all the words right.

I want to be a splendid speller.

Then I stop.

"No, no, no," I say to myself.

I hand in my test to Ms. Glass.

If she knew I peeked,

I bet she would hate me!

At the playground,

I do not play with any kids.

At lunch,

I do not eat my cookies.

I do not sing in music.

At the end of the day,

we get back our tests.

I got one wrong.

"Giggle."

Miss Glass takes me aside.

"What's wrong, Nancy?" she asks.

"Are you upset about the test?

You did very well."

I tell her what I did.

I cry so hard I get hiccups.

"I am a wicked cheater."

Ms. Glass says,

"Nancy, it was wrong

to peek at Bree's paper.

But you did not cheat.

You stopped before you cheated.

I am proud of you for that."

"You are?" I say.

I still feel sad.

S-A-D.

But I do not feel so wicked.

On the way home,

I confess to Bree.

(Confess means telling

something bad you did.)

She forgives me.

She shows me her test.

"I forgot a *p* in 'happy,'" she says.

Maybe we are not always

splendid spellers,

but we are always splendid friends!

Fancy Nancy's Fancy Words

These are the fancy words in this book:

Chien—"dog" in French (you say it like this: SHEE-enn)

Confess—telling someone something bad that you did

Impressed—thinking someone or something is great

Memorize—learn by heart

Splendid—even better than great

Wicked—way worse than bad

Fancy NANCY
Apples Galore!

I adore autumn.

Autumn is a fancy word for fall.

The air is so crisp.

The foliage is so colorful.

Foliage means leaves on the trees.

Ooh la la!

Today our class is going on a trip.

We are going apple picking.

"I hope we pick Gala apples.

My dad likes them best,"

I tell Lionel.

He is my trip buddy.

"A gala is a fancy party.

So Gala apples must be fancy."

Lionel does not answer.

He covers his mouth and gags.

Is he carsick?

Ms. Glass shouts, "Stop the bus!"

Then Lionel laughs and says,

"It was just a joke."

Ms. Glass reprimands Lionel.

That is fancy for scolding.

She often has to reprimand Lionel.

At last we arrive at the orchard.

An orchard is a garden of trees.

Each tree is loaded with apples.

There are apples galore.

"Everyone get a basket.
Remember, do not climb
on branches," Ms. Glass says.
"There are lots of apples
near the ground."

I pick lots of apples.

Lionel juggles apples.

He is an expert juggler.

All of a sudden he stops.

He drops the apples

and runs around in a circle.

"Ow! Ow! Bees are stinging me!"

Ms. Glass dashes over.

That means she hurries to us.

Lionel laughs and says,

"I was just joking!"

"That is not a funny joke,"

Ms. Glass tells him.

She reprimands Lionel some more.

After that, Lionel behaves himself.

We pick lots of apples—apples galore.

We pick Jonathan apples.

We pick Honeycrisp apples.

We do not find a tree with Gala apples.

"Let's look over there," Lionel says,

and he dashes off.

I don't think we should go
so far away.
But trip buddies must stay together.
So I dash after Lionel.

Voilà.

Here are Gala apple trees!

There is one problem.

The apples are on high branches.

A ladder is by another tree.

But Lionel will not help me get it.

He starts climbing up the tree.

"Ms. Glass told us not to,"

I remind him.

Does Lionel listen?

If you said no, you are right!

Up, up he climbs.

Lionel is way out on a branch.

There are so many apples—

Gala apples galore.

Lionel shakes the branch.

The apples do not drop.

He crawls out farther.

"Be careful!" I say.

There is a cracking sound.

Is the branch breaking?

"HELP! HELP!" Lionel yells.

"HELP! HELP!" I yell too.

Kids nearby look over and laugh.

They think it's a joke.

Ms. Glass does not hear us.

She is too far away.

"Can you jump, Lionel?" I ask.

"It's too far down!" he says.

Then I remember the ladder.

I dash over and drag it back.

It is so heavy.

I perspire a lot.

(That is fancy for sweat.)

Ms. Glass is at the tree now.

She sees that this is no joke.

Together we stand up the ladder.

Lionel climbs down to safety.

Crack!

The branch breaks!

Down come the apples.

Ms. Glass is very mad at Lionel.

He cannot go on the hayride.

He cannot help make applesauce.

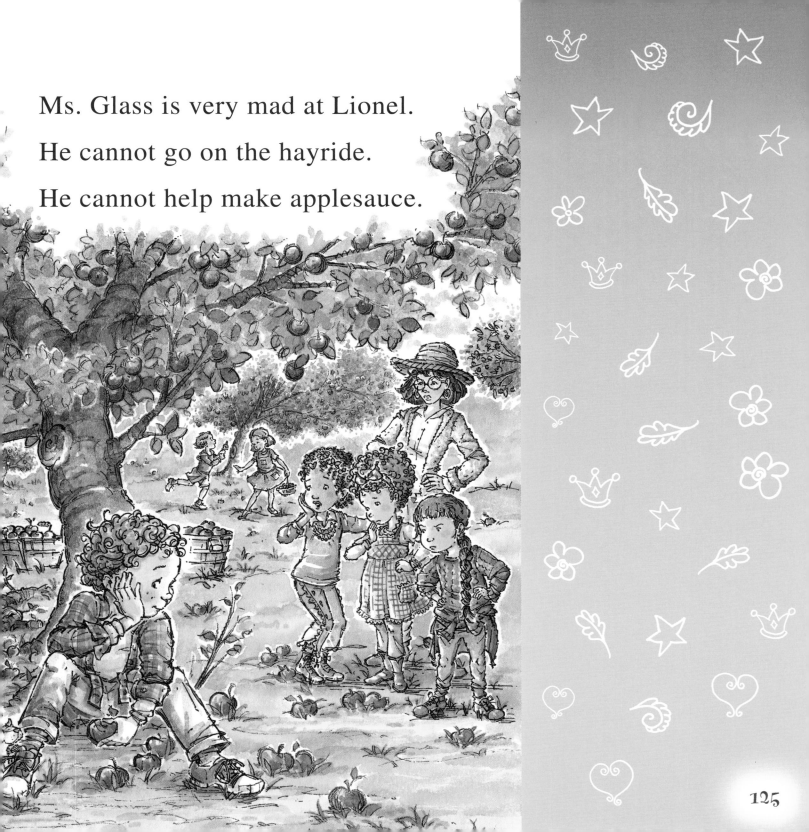

On the ride back I say,

"Thank you for the Gala apples."

I saved some applesauce for Lionel.

He slurps it down and burps.

What a goofball.

Then we each eat a Gala apple.

They do not look fancy.

But they are very tasty.

That's a fancy word for yummy.

There are plenty left for Dad.

Gala apples galore.

Fancy Nancy's Fancy Words

These are the fancy words in this book:

Autumn—fall

Dash—run fast, hurry

Foliage—leaves on the trees

Gala—a fancy party and a kind of apple

Galore—plenty of something

Orchard—a garden of trees

Perspire—sweat

Reprimand—scold

Tasty—yummy

It is the 97th day of school,

and I have a dilemma.

(That is a BIG problem.)

I do not know what to bring in

for the 100th day.

133

Bree put 100 feathers on a hat.

It looks so elegant!

(That's a fancy word for pretty.)

Robert is bringing his stamp album.

There are 100 stamps in it.

Yoko's piggy bank has 100 pennies.

The bank is transparent.

(That means you can see inside.)

Lionel made a ball
out of 100 rubber bands.

After school,

I look all around my room.

I have 39 hair clips.

That is not enough.

I have 57 bracelets.

That is not enough.

I have 84 ribbons.

That is not enough.

What am I going to do?

Now it is the 98th day of school.

More kids bring in stuff:

a bag with 100 marbles,

a jar with 100 jelly beans,

a box with 100 crayons.

I tell Ms. Glass my dilemma.

She tells me not to worry.

"You are very imaginative.

That means you are

full of good ideas.

You will think of something."

At home,

I tell Mom my dilemma.

She is making dinner.

"How about a poster

with macaroni?" she says.

I do not want
to hurt Mom's feelings.
Three kids have already
done stuff with macaroni.
Macaroni is not imaginative.

Dad is doing the wash.

Maybe he will have a good idea.

Dad says,

"I bet we have fifty pairs of socks.

That makes one hundred."

I do not want

to hurt Dad's feelings.

But socks are ugly.

I want something imaginative

and fancy.

After dinner,

I try to think some more.

All of a sudden,

I hear my sister crying.

"Look," my sister says.

She points at her fishbowl.

Goldy is her goldfish.

Goldy is not moving.

We bury Goldy in our yard.

Everyone is sad, even Frenchy.

I am so glad that

dogs live a long time.

We put a few pebbles

from Goldy's bowl on top.

I tell my sister,

"We will remember Goldy fondly."

Fondly means with love.

The next day, I write a poem.

Goldy was gold.

For a fish, she was old.

She liked to swim,

So she stayed slim.

You can't kiss a fish.

But you can miss a fish.

Ms. Glass likes my poem.

She reads it to the class.

"Nancy uses interesting words.

Slim means thin.

Her poem is in verse.

It rhymes."

At home,

it is sad to see the empty fishbowl.

Mom is about to throw out

the pebbles.

Then, all of a sudden,

I get an idea that is imaginative.

"Stop!" I say.

I wash and dry all the pebbles.

They are so pretty.

I count them.

Yes! There are 104!

I get my markers.

I get a huge piece of paper.

Huge is even bigger than big.

I will make a poster.

I spell out Goldy's name
in glitter.

I draw a picture of Goldy
in her bowl.

Then I glue on the pebbles.

I let my sister help.

I write on the poster,

"There are 100 pebbles

in the fishbowl."

Today is the 100th day of school.

I bring in my poster.

I made it just in time!

Ms. Glass brings in something too.

It's a cart with 100 books.

She will read them all to us

before school ends in June.

Ms. Glass is so imaginative!

Fancy Nancy's Fancy Words

These are the fancy words in this book:

Dilemma—a big problem

Elegant—pretty

Fondly—with love

Huge—even bigger than big

Imaginative—full of good ideas

Slim—thin

Transparent—see-through

Verse—a poem that rhymes

Ooh *la la*! Grandma and Grandpa are hosting Thanksgiving dinner this year! After driving for hours, we have finally reached our destination—that's fancy for the place we want to be.

Grandpa opens the door and gives me a giant bear hug. "Bonjour!" we both say. (My grandfather and I love to speak French to each other.)

What a celebration this will be! There is a gigantic turkey, Grandma's secret stuffing, green beans, and authentic cranberry sauce that didn't come out of a can. And desserts? There are almost too many to count.

This is not just a Thanksgiving dinner. This is way fancier. This is a Thanksgiving banquet!

When it is time to eat, I head for the big table.
My mom tells me to go sit at the kids' table—again!
   "But I'm so much more mature than JoJo and my
cousins," I say. (Mature is fancy for grown-up.)
   "I know, but there aren't enough chairs
at our table," Mom says.

I take my place at the kids' table. There are paper plates, paper napkins, and a paper tablecloth. The glasses are plastic. It is not nearly as fancy as the big table, but the food is simply delicious. I am careful to eat with my pinky up and, after each bite, I dab my lips with my napkin. That means I wipe my mouth very gently.

JoJo is not using her party manners! She puts her napkin on her head and makes silly faces. My cousin Arthur laughs so hard he spits out some cranberry juice.

My uncle has to intervene, which means he makes everyone stop acting so immature. "Would it be all right to switch seats with you?" he asks me. "Mais oui! Mais oui! Yes! Yes!" I tell him. "Of course!"

Grandma hands me a fresh napkin with a pretty holder around it.
You can wear it like a bracelet! Très chic! (You say it like this: tray sheek. It means very fancy.)

And the gravy is passed around in a special little boat.

This is more like it.

I am ready for a second helping. I ask politely for the gravy boat. Oh, no! I spill a little by accident.

My grandma says, "I just spilled some cranberry sauce. Don't feel bad. That's what the tablecloth is for."

What a charming hostess my grandma is.

I finish eating way before anybody else. Have you noticed how long it takes grown-ups to eat? And how they only talk about stuff in the news?

"I can spell long words," I tell my aunt. "Like dazzle—d-a-z-z-l-e."
"That's wonderful," my aunt says, but I can tell she is not really interested in spelling.

Ooh! JoJo and my cousins are already starting on dessert. My sister is having apple pie à la mode. (That's French and fancy for "with ice cream.")

JoJo waves to me and takes another bite of pie. "Yummy," she says.

Now everyone at the kids' table is coloring with the new crayons and pads of paper Grandma bought for us. Not to brag, but I am a very talented artist.

"May I be excused?" I ask Mom. I point to the kids' table. "I am going to help them draw stuff."

First I get a plate and sample the desserts.

Then I show everyone how to make butterflies.
(It's easy. You just make a big B together with another
big B that's backwards.)

Because it's Thanksgiving, I also teach them something I learned in school. You trace your hand, and—voilà—soon you have a turkey!

When we are done, we bring our turkeys over to the adults' table.

How to Make a Paper Turkey

1) Trace your hand.
2) Add feathers.
3) Add eyes and a beak.
4) Then fancy it up.
Voilà—a turkey!

"They are wonderful," Grandma and Grandpa tell us. They put the turkeys in the middle of the table, like a centerpiece.

Then Grandpa stands up and says how grateful (that's fancy for being happy and thankful) he is to have the whole family together.

Me, too. I'm so thankful for Thanksgiving.

The END

HarperFestival is an imprint of HarperCollins Publishers.

Fancy Nancy's Fabulous Fall Storybook Collection
Copyright © 2014 by Robin Preiss Glasser and Jane O'Connor

Fancy Nancy: Halloween . . . or Bust! copyright © 2009 by Jane O'Connor
Illustrations copyright © 2009 by Robin Preiss Glasser

Fancy Nancy: Fancy Day in Room 1-A copyright © 2012 by Jane O'Connor
Illustrations copyright © 2012 by Robin Preiss Glasser

Fancy Nancy: Splendid Speller copyright © 2011 by Jane O'Connor
Illustrations copyright © 2011 by Robin Preiss Glasser

Fancy Nancy: Apples Galore! copyright © 2013 by Jane O'Connor
Illustrations copyright © 2013 by Robin Preiss Glasser

Fancy Nancy: The 100th Day of School copyright © 2009 by Jane O'Connor
Illustrations copyright © 2009 by Robin Preiss Glasser

Fancy Nancy: Our Thanksgiving Banquet copyright © 2011 by Jane O'Connor
Illustrations copyright © 2011 by Robin Preiss Glasser

www.harpercollinschildrens.com

ISBN 978-0-06-228884-4
Book Design by Sean Boggs

14 15 16 17 18 SCP 10 9 8 7 6 5 4 3 2 1

❖

First Edition